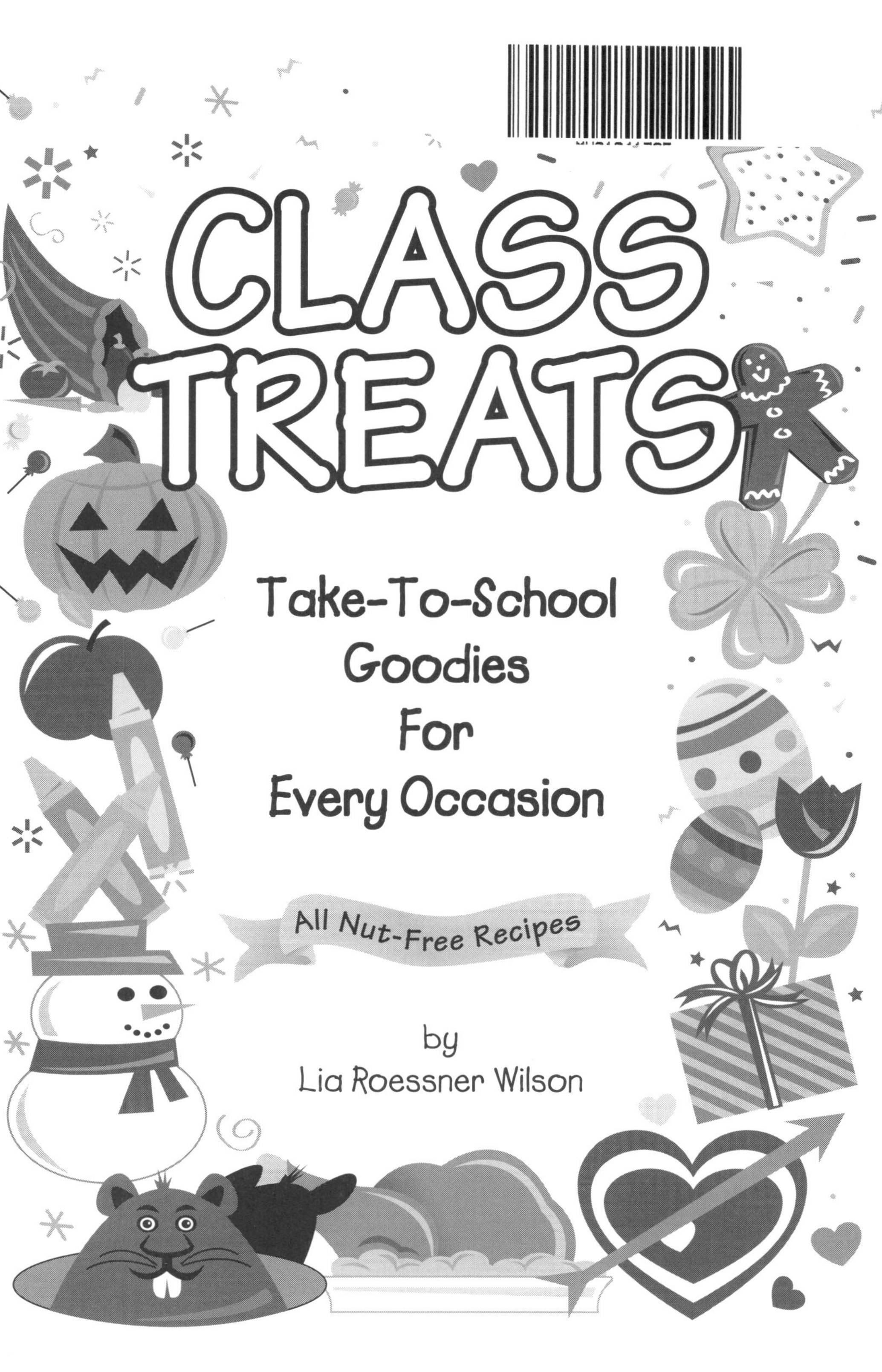

CLASS TREATS

Take-To-School Goodies For Every Occasion

All Nut-Free Recipes

by
Lia Roessner Wilson

Class Treats

1st Printing August 2003
2nd Printing August 2004

ISBN 1-931294-58-5

Library of Congress Number: 2003109820

Art Direction by Liz Reinken
Graphic Design by Fit to Print

Manufactured in China
Edited, Designed and Published in the
United States of America by
Cookbook Resources, LLC
541 Doubletree Drive
Highland Village, Texas 75077
Toll free 866-229-2665
www.cookbookresources.com

FINALLY!

Panic-Free, Last-Minute Treats

As a mother I understand panic from first-hand experience. There's panic one can do something about and then there's panic you have to fight to overcome. Kids' treats and office party sweets fit the first category of panic for me and this cookbook is my answer to the problem.

When one of my boys says there is a party at school the next day or I'm voted to bring refreshments for the office, I no longer panic or go through the related stress and anxiety. There's something about embarrassing your kid not to mention yourself that sends us into these panics. Luckily relief comes not from the drug store, but in your own kitchen pantry.

With just a few basic ingredients, I am able to handle the situation like Betty Crocker herself, only in less time and without all the lights and cameras. And to the relief of my sons, the other kids think their mother is a pretty good cook and that they must not have it too hard at home. What a relief!

So here's the deal. Always have some of these ingredients on hand and this cookbook and your panic attacks are over. Well, maybe a few ingredients and a cookbook will not cure all your panic attacks, but they will certainly take care of kids' treats, office parties and last-minute sweets.

Here are your secret weapons you should always have stashed in the pantry for any emergency:

- 2 (.3 ounce) packages gelatin, several flavors
- 2 (3.4 ounce) packages instant pudding, several flavors
- 2 (18 ounce) boxes cake mix, several flavors
- 2 (16 ounce) cartons ready-to-serve icings, several flavors
- 1 (6 ounce) ready-to-serve pie crust
- Frozen whipped topping
- 2 (20 ounce) cans pie filling, several flavors
- 1 (14 ounce) can sweetened condensed milk
- Chocolate chips
- Ice cream toppings, several flavors

#1

Now, you are set to deal with panic. Read through several pages of this cookbook and put a star by several recipes you want to try for the next ER situation and you are ready. Breath a sigh of relief and go handle some other crisis. You have got this one covered.

Contents

Part 1: STUFF YOU CAN EAT ANY TIME

Part 11: STUFF YOU WANT TO EAT ALL THE TIME

Part I:

Stuff You Can Eat Any Time

Trail Mix

Trail Mix makes a handy snack you can help yourself to any time. Store in an airtight container or divide into single servings and store in sealable plastic bags. Use your imagination for other ingredients to add.

1 cup rice, oat, corn, rice or wheat cereal
1 cup chopped dried fruit
1 cup chocolate chips
1 cup raisins
1 cup shredded coconut

★ Mix together in airtight container.

★ Substitute or add other favorite ingredients.

Gravel Sticks

These chocolate-dipped pretzels could not be easier. Vary the coatings for more festive looks. Try white chocolate with crushed red and green peppermint candies or colored candy sprinkles.

2 cups (one 12-ounce package) semi-sweet or milk chocolate chips
1 tablespoon cooking oil or shortening
2 cups crushed malted milk balls
1 (10 ounce package) pretzel rods (about ½-inch in diameter)

★ Combine chocolate chips and shortening in microwave-safe bowl or dish.

★ Heat on HALF power for several minutes, stirring after each minute, until mixture melts. Stir mixture until smooth.

★ Put crushed milk balls onto shallow plate or tray. Break each pretzel rod in half, dip broken end into chocolate and roll in crushed malted milk balls.

★ Set on wax paper or foil-lined baking sheet and refrigerate until chocolate is set.

Pumpkin Seeds

Here's a fun way to use the seeds from your Halloween pumpkin carvings. Flavor and roast the pumpkin seeds for a crunchy treat.

3 tablespoons butter or margarine, melted
1/2 teaspoon worchestershire sauce
1/2 teaspoon garlic powder
1 teaspoon salt
1 1/2-2 cups pumpkin seeds, rinsed, dried

★ Preheat oven to 350°. Put melted butter in large bowl and stir in worchestershire sauce, garlic powder and salt.

★ Add pumpkin seeds to butter mixture and stir well to coat.

★ Place seeds in single layer on baking sheet and sprinkle with salt.

★ Bake for 12 to 15 minutes, stirring occasionally, until seeds are brown and crispy.

Easy Corn Nuts Brittle

This microwave recipe uses Corn Nuts (roasted, crunchy corn snacks) instead of peanuts for a totally different taste and a nut-free candy. It is a fun recipe for kids to help with, but special care should be taken because the brittle mixture gets extremely hot.

1 cup sugar
½ cup white corn syrup
1 cup Corn Nuts
1 teaspoon butter or margarine
1 teaspoon vanilla
1 teaspoon baking soda

★ Lightly grease baking sheet and place in 200° oven until ready to use.

★ Mix sugar and corn syrup in 1½-quart casserole dish. Microwave on HIGH for 4 minutes.

★ Stir in Corn Nuts and microwave again on HIGH for 4 minutes or until light brown.

★ Stir butter and vanilla into syrup mixture and mix well. Microwave on HIGH for 2 minutes.

★ Add baking soda and stir quickly until mixture is light and foamy.

★ Quickly pour mixture onto prepared baking sheet and spread thinly with buttered spatula or back of spoon.

★ Let brittle cool. Break into pieces and store in an airtight container.

Alphabet Pretzels

Try using cinnamon and sugar on these in place of salt for a sweet alternative.

2 (16 ounce) loaves frozen bread dough, thawed
1 egg white, slightly beaten
1 teaspoon water
1/4 cup coarse salt

★ Divide each loaf into 12 pieces. Roll each piece into rope about 12 inches long.

★ Shape bread ropes into letter or number shapes and place 1 inch apart on greased baking sheet. Cover lightly with plastic wrap and let stand for 20 minutes.

★ Preheat oven at 350°.

★ Combine egg white and water in small bowl.

★ Using soft pastry brush, lightly brush each bread shape with combined egg white and water. Sprinkle with coarse salt.

★ Put shallow pan containing boiling water in bottom of oven.

★ Bake pretzels on rack above water for 20 minutes or until golden brown.

Cheesy Puff Balls

2 cups flour
1 cup (2 sticks) butter or margarine
$1^1/_2$ cups shredded sharp cheddar cheese

★ Preheat oven to 400°.

★ Cream flour, butter and cheese together in large bowl.

★ Roll pieces of dough into $1^1/_2$-inch balls. Place 2 inches apart on lightly greased baking sheet.

★ Bake for 10 to 15 minutes or until golden brown. Let cool.

★ Makes about 4 to 5 dozen.

Tip: You may also freeze these instead of baking them and keep them frozen until you're ready to serve.

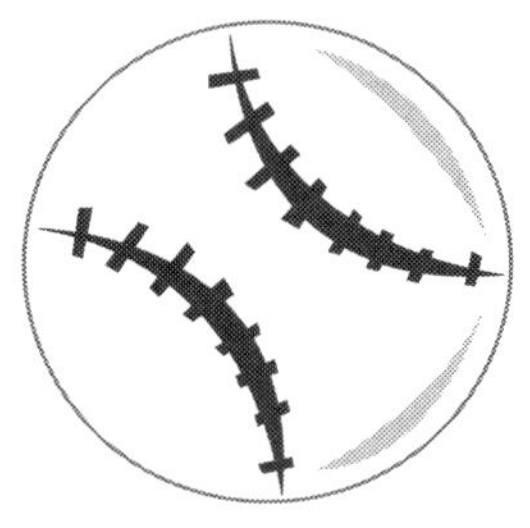

Cottage Cheese Dip

Make this easy, tasty cheese dip to serve with favorite fresh vegetable sticks like celery, carrots, broccoli and tomato slices.

$^1/_2$ package onion or vegetable soup mix
$^1/_3$ cup milk
1 pint cottage cheese

★ Put soup mix, milk and cottage cheese in bowl and stir well to mix.

★ Cover and refrigerate for 30 minutes or until cold. Serve with crackers, chips or vegetable sticks.

Cream Cheese Island Dip

1 (8 ounce) package cream cheese, softened
1 (12 ounce) jar picante sauce
1 bag tortilla chips

★ Place cream cheese in bowl and cover with picante sauce.

★ Dip chips into picante sauce and cream cheese together.

Sandwich Pinwheels

To make this a little different, use flavored cream cheeses, such as blueberry or strawberry, in place of the pimiento cheese.

Bread slices
Pimiento cheese spread or flavored cream cheese

★ Cut crusts off bread slices.

★ Roll each bread slice flat with rolling pin and cover with thin layer of pimiento cheese spread or flavored cream cheese.

★ Roll in jelly-roll fashion and cut into 1-inch pieces.

Fun Food Shapes

Use large cookie cutters to create lots of fun foods for kids. Metal cookie cutters have sharp edges making it easy to cut shapes. These recipes are fun to do all year long because you will be able to find a suitable cookie cutter for every season and occasion.

French Toast Shapes

These are great for kids, but also nice for Valentine's Day breakfast with heart-shaped toast and strawberries on the side!

1 egg
2 tablespoons milk
1 teaspoon sugar
¼ teaspoon vanilla
Pinch salt
5 slices sandwich bread
1 tablespoon butter or margarine

★ Beat egg and milk together, then beat in sugar, vanilla and salt.
★ Place bread slices on flat surface and cut shapes out of each slice of bread using cookie cutters.
★ Heat butter in skillet over medium heat until it melts and simmers.
★ Dip each bread shape into egg mixture, coating 1 side first and then the other.
★ Place in skillet and let cook for 1 to 2 minutes or until browned. Turn and cook other side.
★ Serve with pancake syrup or powdered sugar.

(continued on next page)

(continued)

Pancake Shapes

Use heat-resistant metal cookie cutters with rubber grips to handle these shapes.

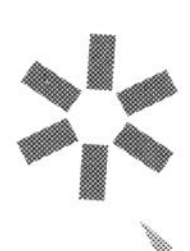

Pancake mix
Milk
Butter
Syrup

★ Spray griddle and cookie cutter's edge inside and out. Set in pan and pour a few tablespoons pancake batter inside.
★ Leave cookie cutter in place until bubbles pop on top of pancake, leaving little "craters".
★ Gently lift cookie cutter with rubber handle tongs or hot pad.
★ Flip pancake shape over to cook other side.

Cinnamon Toast Shapes

2 tablespoons sugar
2 teaspoons cinnamon
4 slices bread
4 tablespoons butter or margarine

★ Preheat oven to 350°.
★ Mix sugar and cinnamon together in small bowl and set aside.
★ Cut shapes out of bread slices with cookie cutters.
★ Spread each piece of bread generously with butter and sprinkle cinnamon-sugar mixture over top.
★ Place under broiler to toast until butter and sugar melt and bubble.

(continued on next page)

(continued)

Sandwich Shapes

Bread slices
Lunch meat slices
Cheese slices
Mayonnaise or sandwich spread
Fresh fruit

★ Use cookie cutter to cut shapes out of slices of bread, lunch meat and cheese.
★ Spread bread with mayonnaise or sandwich spread and build sandwiches with slices of cheese and lunch meat.
★ Serve with fresh fruit.

Cheese Toast Shapes

Bread slices
Cheese slices

★ Preheat oven or broiler to 350°.
★ Cut shapes from bread and cheese with cookie cutter.
★ Place bread shapes on baking sheet and put matching slice of cheese on each.
★ Put baking sheet in oven until cheese melts.

(continued on next page)

(continued)

Ice Cream Shapes

By choosing different flavored ice creams, you may match holiday colors. For example, green mint ice cream for Christmas trees and cherry ice cream for Valentine's Day hearts.

2-3 baking sheets with low sides
1 quart ice cream

- ★ Freeze 2 or 3 baking sheets for several hours to keep ice cream from melting quickly.
- ★ Soften ice cream quickly by microwaving it at HALF power for 3 to 5 minutes or until it reaches spreading consistency.
- ★ Remove one frozen baking sheet from freezer and spread softened ice cream evenly over bottom. Freeze ice cream until very firm.
- ★ Remove from freezer. Cut shapes using cookie cutters and place cut-outs on another frozen baking sheet. Put leftover ice cream 'scraps' in container and refreeze.
- ★ Work fast so ice cream shapes do not melt. If needed, work in batches to make a few at a time, refreeze and make more later.
- ★ Serve shapes on cold plates and decorate each with chocolate topping or colorful candy sprinkles. You may also serve each shape on slice of pound cake and top with sauce or sprinkles.

Cinnamon Snails

4 slices soft-texture bread, crusts removed
1/4 cup cream cheese, softened
3 tablespoons sugar
1 1/2 teaspoons cinnamon
1/4 cup (1/2 stick) butter or margarine, melted

★ Preheat oven to 350°.

★ Spread each slice of bread with 1 tablespoon cream cheese.

★ Roll up bread slices jelly-roll fashion with cream cheese on the inside. Cut each roll into thirds.

★ In small bowl, mix sugar and cinnamon. Dip each roll into melted butter (don't dip the ends), then into sugar-cinnamon mixture.

★ Place rolls, seam side down, on ungreased baking sheet.

★ Bake for 12 minutes or until light brown and crisp.

Squiggly Worms

1 (6 ounce) package raspberry gelatin
3 (.25 ounce) packets unflavored gelatin
3 cups boiling water
100 plastic straws
1 (1 quart) empty milk or orange juice container
$^{3}/_{4}$ cup whipping cream
12-15 drops red food coloring

★ In large bowl, combine raspberry and unflavored gelatin. Add boiling water and stir until gelatin dissolves. Cover and chill about 20 minutes until lukewarm.

★ Place straws in tall container.

★ Blend cream and food coloring into lukewarm gelatin mixture. Pour into straws to fill them.

★ Chill at least 8 hours until gelatin is firm.

★ Remove straws from container and separate. Run hot water over straws for 1 to 2 seconds.

★ Starting at empty end squeeze between fingers and push worms from straws. Place worms on wax paper-lined baking sheets.

★ Cover and chill at least 1 hour until ready to use. (Worms can stay in refrigerator for up to 2 days.) Worms will keep solid at room temperature for up to 2 hours.

Chocolate-Covered Marshmallows

For a festive holiday look and taste, roll these treats in crushed peppermints while the chocolate is still wet. It is easy in the microwave.

1 cup semi-sweet or milk chocolate chips
¼ cup shortening
1 (10 ounce) package large marshmallows
50 toothpicks

★ Place chocolate chips and shortening in large microwave-safe measuring cup.

★ Microwave on HALF power for 1 to 3 minutes or until chips are shiny and soft. Stir chocolate and butter until mixture is smooth.

★ Stick toothpick into marshmallow and dip marshmallow into chocolate, rolling it around until it is completely covered.

★ Put marshmallows on wax paper until chocolate dries. Serve with toothpick.

Crunchy Clouds

1 (14 ounce) package caramels, unwrapped
1 (14 ounce) can sweetened condensed milk
1/2 cup (1 stick) butter or margarine
1 cup crisped rice cereal
1 (10 ounce) bag large marshmallows

★ Put caramels, milk and butter in heavy saucepan over low heat. Stir and cook until butter melts and mixture is smooth.

★ Remove saucepan from heat. Use fork to spear each marshmallow and dip into caramel mixture. Roll in crisped rice cereal.

★ Set on wax paper or foil until chocolate dries.

Chocolate Popcorn

12 cups popped popcorn
1 cup corn syrup
$^{1}/_{4}$ cup ($^{1}/_{2}$ stick) butter or margarine
2 cups milk chocolate chips

★ Preheat oven at 300°. Place popcorn in 9 x 13-inch greased roasting pan.

★ Combine corn syrup, butter and chocolate chips in heavy saucepan over medium heat. Cook, stirring constantly, until mixture comes to a boil.

★ Remove from heat and pour over popcorn. Stir well to coat.

★ Bake for 45 minutes, stirring every 15 minutes. Remove from oven and let cool. Store in airtight container.

Honey Popcorn

6 cups popped popcorn
1 cup miniature chocolate chips or candy-coated chocolate
1/2 cup honey
1/2 cup (1 stick) butter or margarine

★ Preheat oven to 350°.

★ Combine popcorn and chocolate pieces in large bowl and set aside.

★ Put honey and butter in saucepan over medium-low heat. Cook until butter melts and mixture is smooth.

★ Pour honey mixture over popcorn and chocolate, stirring to coat. When coated, spread in single layer in 9 x 13-inch baking dish.

★ Bake for 5 to10 minutes, stirring occasionally, until popcorn is crisp.

★ Remove from oven and let cool. Store in airtight container or in resealable plastic bags.

Christmas Popcorn "Ornaments"

These marshmallow-flavored popcorn balls look pretty in Christmas colors. They are so easy and fast to make, make one batch in green and another in red. For added fun, use red licorice lace to make a loop on top. Cut a piece about 8 inches long, fold in half and put loose ends in popcorn ball when you make it.

5 cups popped popcorn
2 tablespoons margarine, softened
3 cups miniature marshmallows
5 drops red or green food coloring

★ Spray inside large mixing bowl with nonstick cooking spray or grease it with margarine.

★ Put popcorn and chocolate chips in prepared bowl.

★ Place margarine and marshmallows in 4-cup microwave-safe measuring cup and microwave on HIGH power for 1 minute, add food coloring and stir until mixture is smooth. If necessary, microwave for another 30 seconds to 1 minute.

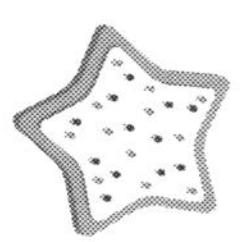

(continued on next page)

(continued)

★ Pour marshmallow mixture over popcorn and stir quickly to coat.

★ Butter your hands and shape mixture into balls. Place on wax paper. Let stand for 1 hour.

Makes 6 to 8 balls.

Tip: If you want to save time, you can purchase popped popcorn in bags at your grocery store.

Rudolph Heads

Pound cake
Chocolate frosting
Raisins
Candy cherry halves
Broken pretzels

★ Slice pound cake into 1-inch slices.

★ Spread frosting on each slice of pound cake and cut in half diagonally.

★ Put cherry half on one corner of the triangle to make reindeer nose.

★ Put raisins above to make eyes.

★ Place broken pretzel piece on each of two corners above eyes to make antlers.

Ho Ho Ho

Warm-Me-Up Cider

The following recipe makes 1 individual serving. Repeat steps for as many servings as needed.

1 cup apple cider
2 teaspoons honey
Pinch cinnamon

★ Pour apple cider or apple juice into microwave-safe mug or glass measuring cup.

★ Stir honey and cinnamon into cider.

★ Microwave on HIGH for 2 minutes or until cider is hot. Stir and serve.

Hot Cocoa Mix

Make hot chocolate mix and keep it on hand to have a cup whenever you want!

1 (16 ounce) box powdered sugar
1 (2 pound) box Nestle Quick
1 (6 ounce) can coffee creamer
1 (8 quart) box powdered milk

★ Mix powdered sugar, Nestle Quick, coffee creamer and powdered milk together in large bowl and store in airtight container.

★ To serve, put 1/2 cup mix in mug, add hot water and stir.

Ruby Fizz

1 1/2 cups cranberry juice
3 scoops raspberry sherbet
1/2 cup ginger ale

★ Pour all ingredients into blender.

★ Cover and blend until mixture is very smooth.

★ Pour into glasses and share!

Ghoulish Green Punch

Serve this frightfully good drink at your next Halloween party!

1 (.14 ounce) package unsweetened lime-flavored drink mix
4 cups water
3/4 cup sugar
2 1/2 cups pineapple juice
1/4 cup lime juice
1 (2 liter) bottle lemon-lime flavored soda or ginger ale

★ Mix all ingredients together in large bowl and chill.

★ To serve immediately, refrigerate all liquid ingredients before mixing.

Frothy Fruit

1 banana
2 cups strawberry yogurt
1 cup frozen strawberries
1 cup orange juice

★ Peel banana, wrap in plastic wrap and freeze for 2 hours.

★ Put yogurt, strawberries, frozen banana and orange juice into blender.

★ Puree until all ingredients are smooth and frothy. Pour into glasses and serve.

Makes 3 or 4 servings.

Berry Delicious Smoothie

1 ripe banana, sliced
1 cup milk
½ cup strawberry yogurt
4 ice cubes

★ Put banana slices, milk, yogurt and ice cubes in blender.

★ Blend for about 30 seconds or until mixture is smooth. Pour into glasses.

Makes 2 servings.

Banana Monkey

2 ripe bananas, sliced
½ cup milk
1½ cups vanilla ice cream
¼ cup chocolate syrup

★ Put bananas, milk, ice cream and chocolate syrup into blender on high speed for about 30 seconds or until mixture is smooth. Pour into glasses.

Makes 2 to 3 servings.

Polar Pops

1 cup orange or apple juice
1 cup cranberry juice

★ Put orange juice and cranberry juice in bowl and stir well.

★ Pour juice into each of 4 small paper cups.

★ Cover each cup tightly with foil. Insert wooden craft stick (popsicle stick) through foil in center of each cup.

★ Put cups in freezer until mixture is solid. When frozen, peel cup away and serve.

Tropical Popsicles

2 cups lemon yogurt
$^{1}/_{2}$ cup crushed pineapple, drained
1 (6 ounce) can orange-pineapple juice concentrate, thawed

★ Combine all ingredients in bowl and mix well.

★ Spoon mixture into 4 small paper cups.

★ Cover each cup tightly with plastic wrap or foil.

★ Insert wooden craft stick (popsicle stick) into each cup through plastic wrap or foil so that it stands up straight.

★ Put cups in freezer until mixture is solid. Remove plastic wrap and peel away paper cup to serve.

Frozen Yogurt Pops

1 (8 ounce) carton strawberry yogurt
1 cup sliced bananas
1 tablespoon sugar

★ Put yogurt, banana slices and sugar in blender and puree for about 30 seconds or until mixture is smooth and blended.

★ Put mixture into covered container and freeze for 30 minutes.

★ Blend again and spoon mixture into 3 or 4 very small paper cups.

★ Cover each cup tightly with foil and insert wooden craft stick (popsicle stick) in center and freeze for another hour until solid.

★ Peel cup away and serve.

Pink Pops

2 cups plain yogurt
1 (12 ounce) can cranberry-apple juice concentrate

★ Combine yogurt with juice concentrate and pour into 8 small paper cups.

★ Insert wooden craft stick or plastic spoon in middle of each for handle.

★ Freeze until set. Peel cups away and serve.

Frozen Gems

Fill a glass with sparkling ice cube juice gems that flavor and color the clear soda as they melt.

Assorted fruit juices

★ Pour several different colored juices into ice cube trays and freeze.

★ When juice is frozen, place several colored cubes in clear glass and pour white grape juice or lemon-lime flavored soda over colored cubes.

★ As cubes melt, they will color and flavor juice or soda.

Slushy Peaches

$^{1}/_{2}$ cup milk
1 cup sliced fresh or canned peaches
1 teaspoon sugar

★ Pour milk into ice cube tray and freeze until solid.

★ Remove frozen milk cubes from tray and place in blender. Add peaches and sugar.

★ Cover and blend on high speed until mixture is smooth. Serve immediately.

Wormy Apples

6 large apples
4 ounces raspberry jam
2 tablespoons butter or margarine
6 gummy worms

★ Preheat oven to 350°.

★ Core apples from stem end to within ½-inch from bottom. Leave bottoms intact so apples will hold filling.

★ Fill center of each apple with 1 teaspoon jam and 1 teaspoon butter.

★ Place apples in 9 x 13-inch baking dish and bake uncovered for 35 to 45 minutes or until apples are fork-tender but not mushy.

★ Remove apples from oven and cool 15 minutes.

★ Put each apple in bowl and spoon syrup from baking pan onto each apple. Place gummy worm in top of each apple and leave half body visible.

Icy Orange Bowls

4 oranges
1 pint orange sherbet
4 maraschino cherries

★ Cut tops off the oranges and carefully hollow out insides.

★ Set orange rinds in muffin tins and fill each with large scoop of orange sherbet. Top sherbet with cherry and put in freezer for 2 to 3 hours.

★ Before serving remove from freezer and thaw for 5 minutes to soften.

Easy Caramel Apples

1 (14 ounce) package caramels, unwrapped
1 cup miniature marshmallows
1 tablespoon water
6 wooden craft sticks
5-6 small apples, washed, dried

★ Line baking sheet with foil or wax paper and set aside.

★ Combine caramels, marshmallows and water in medium saucepan. Cook over medium heat, stirring constantly, until caramels melt.

★ Remove from heat and cool slightly.

★ While caramel mixture is cooling, insert wooden craft stick into each apple.

★ Dip apples one by one in caramel mixture to coat completely. Place on prepared baking sheet to set. Refrigerate until firm.

Fruit Kabobs

1 tangerine, peeled
1 apple
1 banana
1 cup seedless grapes
4 or 5 wooden skewers

★ Divide tangerine into sections.

★ Slice apple and banana into pieces about 1/2-inch thick.

★ Arrange different kinds fruits on 4 wooden skewers.

★ Spoon Kabob Dip (page 41) over them and serve.

Kabob Dip

1 (8 ounce) package cream cheese, softened
1/2 cup packed brown sugar
1 teaspoon finely shredded orange peel
1 teaspoon vanilla

★ Put cream cheese, brown sugar, orange peel and vanilla in bowl. Mix well and serve.

Speedy Fruit Salad

2 (8 ounce) cartons strawberry yogurt
1/4 cup raisins
1 orange or tangerine, peeled, separated into segments
1 banana, sliced
Lemon juice

★ Mix yogurt, raisins and orange together in large bowl and chill in refrigerate.

★ Just before serving, peel banana, slice and squirt with lemon juice. Stir into salad and serve.

Arctic Bananas

4 cups milk, divided
1 (3½ ounce) package instant vanilla pudding mix
2 bananas, mashed
1 (4½ ounce) package instant chocolate pudding mix

- ★ In bowl, mix 2 cups milk with vanilla pudding and beat well.
- ★ Stir in mashed bananas and whisk mixture using fork or wire whisk until blended.
- ★ In another bowl, combine remaining milk and chocolate pudding mix and beat until well blended.
- ★ Divide half banana pudding mixture between 18 paper cups and spoon layer of chocolate pudding over banana mixture.
- ★ Spoon remaining banana mixture over chocolate pudding. Take butter knife and swirl it through mixture in cups to create marbled effect.
- ★ Put wooden craft stick (popsicle stick) in center of each cup and put cups in the freezer for several hours. When the mixture is frozen, peel away drink cups and serve.

Banana Dips

Use bananas that are just ripe (not mushy).

1/2 cup shredded coconut, toasted
1/2 cup candy sprinkles
4 ripe bananas, peeled
8 wooden craft sticks
1/2 cup honey

- ★ Spread toasted coconut on 1 plate and candy sprinkles on another.
- ★ Cut bananas in half across middle. Insert craft stick into each cut end.
- ★ Hold each banana half over plate or wax paper to catch drips and pour a little honey over it, smoothing honey with back of spoon to coat all sides.
- ★ Roll honey-coated banana in candy sprinkles, coconut or both to coat on all sides.
- ★ Place banana on wax paper-lined baking sheet. Repeat with remaining bananas.

Frozen Chocolate-Covered Bananas

6 large ripe bananas
2 cups semi-sweet or milk chocolate chips
2 tablespoons vegetable shortening

- ★ Peel each banana and cut in half crosswise. Insert wooden craft stick into cut end of each half.
- ★ Wrap and freeze each banana for at least 1 hour.
- ★ Line baking sheet with foil and refrigerate to chill.
- ★ When ready to cover bananas, melt chocolate chips and shortening together in small, heavy saucepan over low heat. Stir until mixture is smooth.
- ★ Remove bananas from freezer and dip them into warm chocolate. Cover bananas completely and let excess chocolate drip off.
- ★ Place on chilled baking sheet. Cover with wax paper and return to freezer until chocolate is hard.
- ★ Before serving, let bananas sit, covered, at room temperature for 20 to 30 minutes.

Chocolate-Banana Sandwiches

1 (16 ounce) pound cake
1 (16 ounce) carton chocolate frosting
5-6 bananas

★ Slice cake into 1/2-inch slices.

★ Place slice on plate and cover with chocolate frosting.

★ Slice bananas and put in single layer over chocolate frosting.

★ Cover another slice of cake with frosting and place it frosting side down over bananas. Repeat for as many sandwiches as you want.

Banana S'mores

Enjoy these over a campfire or bake them in the oven at home. They are delicious any way you make them.

4 unpeeled bananas
1/2 cup miniature chocolate chips
3/4 cup miniature marshmallows

★ Peel each banana down 1 side only but don't remove peel.

★ Cut wedge out of banana in peeled area.

★ Sprinkle some chocolate chips into wedge and cover with marshmallows.

★ Replace peel and wrap banana in aluminum foil.

★ Put into coals for about 5 minutes or place in oven at 350° for 5 to 7 minutes or until chocolate melts and marshmallows are toasted.

Strawberry Ladybugs

1 pint large strawberries
8 thin pretzel sticks for each strawberry
$^1/_2$ cup chocolate chips
1 tablespoon butter or margarine
Several teaspoonfuls miniature chocolate chips

★ Wash and dry strawberries. Remove stems and cut in half from stem to tip.

★ Melt chocolate chips and butter in small saucepan over low heat or in microwave on HALF power. Stir until smooth.

★ Place 4 pretzels with ends just touching on foil-lined baking sheet. Space outer ends of pretzels so they look like legs.

★ Dip cut side of strawberries in chocolate and place on top of pretzels.

★ Carefully dip miniature chocolate chips in melted chocolate (for "glue") and stick on strawberry for ladybug spots.

Frozen Fruit Cupcakes

Fresh strawberries, blueberries, raspberries and cherries are great in this frozen surprise.

1 pint orange or lemon sherbet
1 (12 ounce) bag mixed frozen berries or 2 cups assorted fresh fruit, divided

★ Melt sherbet in large bowl.

★ Line muffin tins with 12 foil baking cups

★ Cut larger pieces of fruit (like strawberries) into smaller pieces, if necessary. Stir 1 1/4 cups frozen fruit into sherbet.

★ Spoon sherbet mixture into baking cups. Arrange remaining 3/4 cup fruit on top.

★ Cover with plastic wrap and put in freezer for about 3 hours or until frozen solid. Peel away baking cups and serve.

Creamy Fruit Parfaits

A parfait is a layered dessert. Use dessert glasses, nice wine glasses or even clear plastic cups to see the colorful layers in this delicious dessert.

1 (8 ounce) package cream cheese, softened
1 (7 ounce) jar marshmallow cream
1 cup sliced strawberries
1 cup blueberry pie filling

★ Mix cream cheese and marshmallow cream together in bowl until smooth.

★ Divide cream cheese mixture in half and spoon in 4 dessert cups or glasses. Divide strawberries among cups, layering on top of cream cheese mixture.

★ Put remaining cream cheese mixture over strawberries in each glass.

★ Top each with blueberry pie filling.

Bear Biscuits

1 tablespoon butter or margarine
1 (10 ounce) can buttermilk biscuits
12 raisins

★ Preheat oven at 400°.

★ Lightly grease baking sheet.

★ Separate biscuits and cut 3 into sixths for ears and noses and leave 6 biscuits whole for heads.

★ Form heads by rolling each whole biscuit into ball, place on baking sheet and flatten slightly.

★ Roll 3 small pieces of dough into balls. Place 1 on either side of top of ball for ears and 1 into center of head for the nose.

★ Press 2 raisins into the dough for nose and eyes.

★ Bake for 8 to10 minutes or until golden brown.

Cinnamon Spirals

1 (10 ounce) can refrigerated biscuits
$^1/_2$ cup (1 stick) butter or margarine
1 cup sugar
1 teaspoon cinnamon

★ Preheat oven at 350°.

★ Working with 1 biscuit at a time, stretch it into a 3 x 4-inch oval.

★ Melt butter and set aside.

★ In small bowl, combine cinnamon and sugar and mix well.

★ Working with 1 biscuit at a time, dip biscuit into melted butter and coat both sides.

★ Dip biscuit into cinnamon-sugar mixture and cover completely.

★ Twist coated biscuit about 3 or 4 times in one direction and place on baking sheet.

★ Bake for about 15 minutes or until golden brown.

Strawberry Butter

This fancy butter for pancakes or biscuits is a tasty spread especially nice around Valentine's Day.

1 (16 ounce) package frozen strawberries, thawed
1 pound butter, softened
$^1/_2$ cup powdered sugar

★ Put strawberries and butter in bowl and beat with hand mixer on medium speed until smooth.

★ Gradually add sugar and continue beating until well blended.

Breakfast Burritos

This hot, hearty breakfast dish is easy to eat and easy to take on the road if you're in a hurry. Just wrap it in a paper towel and go.

Flour tortillas
1 egg per tortilla
1/4 cup shredded cheddar cheese per tortilla
1-2 slices bacon per tortilla, cooked, crumbled
Salsa, optional

★ Scramble eggs and add crumbled bacon or diced ham.

★ Spoon into middle of flour tortilla and top with cheese and salsa.

★ Fold one side over filling and roll to keep filling inside.

Sandwich Spirals

1 apple, peeled, cored, coarsely chopped
1/4 cup raisins or chopped dates
1/3 cup honey
1 tablespoon lemon juice
1 teaspoon ground cinnamon
Several slices sandwich bread

★ Place apple pieces, raisins, honey, lemon juice and cinnamon in food processor and process until mixture is smooth.

★ Lay piece of bread on plate and spread about 1 tablespoon of mixture over it.

★ Roll bread jelly-roll fashion. Cut into slices about 1-inch thick. Repeat with remaining bread slices and filling.

Happy Faces

Chalupa shells are flat crispy taco shells. They work great for this dish because they're rigid and flat. If they aren't available, flour tortillas work fine. Once your artistic handiwork has been seen and appreciated, they can be folded like a taco and eaten!

Soft flour tortillas or chalupa shells
Refried beans
Shredded cheddar cheese or lettuce for hair
Sliced black olives for eyes
Green olive half for nose
Tomato slice for mouth

★ Spread each tortilla or chalupa shell with refried beans.

★ Sprinkle shredded cheese or lettuce at top for hair and position 2 olive slices for eyes. Use green olive half for nose. Put tomato slice for mouth.

Pizza Bites

These fast little snacks can be jazzed up with parmesan cheese or Italian seasonings if you want stronger flavors.

Tomato paste
Shredded mozzarella cheese
Pepperoni slices or sliced weiners

★ Spread tomato paste over crackers and place them on baking sheet.

★ Top each with slice of pepperoni or slice of weiner. Sprinkle cheese on top.

★ Broil for 1 or 2 minutes until cheese melt and bubbles.

Salad Sea Shells

Here is a fun and different way to serve sandwich fillings.

8 jumbo pasta shells
1 cup tuna, chicken or egg salad
$^1/_2$ cup grated cheese, optional

★ Cook pasta shells according to package directions. Rinse in cold water and drain well.

★ Fill each shell with tuna or egg salad and sprinkle with grated cheese, if desired.

Tangy Chicken

This tasty chicken dish is a snap to make because it takes only a couple of minutes to mix the tangy sauce. It works best if you cook the chicken on a rack so that the sauce isn't diluted by the chicken juices. (It tastes great on pork too.)

6-8 skinless, boneless chicken breasts
1 package dry onion soup mix
1 (10 ounce) jar apricot preserves
1 (8 ounce) bottle Russian dressing

★ Place chicken in single layer in 9 x 13-inch baking dish.

★ In bowl, combine onion soup mix, apricot preserves and Russian dressing. Pour over chicken.

★ Bake uncovered at 350° for 45 minutes.

Soft Chicken Tacos

These are super easy to put together when you keep the ingredients on hand in the refrigerator.

4 boneless skinless chicken breasts, cooked, diced
1 pound bacon, cooked, crumbled
1 tomato, diced
Shredded lettuce
1 cup shredded Monterey Jack cheese
1 (8 ounce) bottle ranch-style dressing
Soft flour tortillas

★ Combine chicken, bacon, tomato, lettuce and cheese. Stir until well mixed.

★ Pour dressing over and toss.

★ Spoon some of chicken mixture into center of tortilla and fold over.

Crunchy Chicken Fingers

1/4 cup honey, warmed
1/4 cup water
1 cup crushed corn flakes
3-4 skinless, boneless chicken breasts

★ Preheat oven to 425°.

★ Spray baking sheet with vegetable spray.

★ Mix honey and water together in small bowl.

★ Put corn flakes on plate.

★ Cut chicken breasts into strips 3/4-inch wide.

★ Dip each chicken strip in honey mixture and dredge in corn flake crumbs to coat. Place on baking sheet.

★ Bake for 10 to 12 minutes or until cooked. Turn each piece midway during cooking.

Pigs In A Blanket

Cheddar cheese with sausages give this version of the perennial favorite a nice twist. Not only will your kids love it, but you will also. It makes a nice snack that everyone can enjoy.

1 package (8 count) refrigerated crescent rolls
8 slices cheddar or American cheese
16 Little Smokies sausages

★ Preheat oven to 375°.

★ Cut cheese slices in half diagonally to make 2 triangles.

★ Lay crescent roll out on ungreased baking sheet and flatten slightly.

★ Place 1 cheese triangle on crescent roll, fitting it into shape of dough.

★ Place 2 sausages side by side on cheese.

★ Roll up, starting with long side of dough triangle. Lift corners over to middle of roll and pinch edges to seal. Repeat with remaining rolls and ingredients.

★ Bake for 10 to 12 minutes or until golden brown.

Fish In A River

You can also use flavored cream cheese in this recipe.

4 celery sticks
1 (3 ounce) package cream cheese, softened
2-3 drops blue food coloring
20-25 goldfish crackers

★ Wash celery and cut it into pieces about 4-inches long.

★ In small bowl, combine cream cheese and food coloring. Mix until cream cheese is completely blue.

★ Use butter knife to spread cream cheese into hollow part of each celery stick.

★ Place 3 or 4 goldfish crackers on cream cheese in each stick and gently press them into cheese.

No-Bowl Frito Pie

Can you eat chili without a bowl? You bet!

Heated chili
Single-size bag Fritos
Shredded cheddar cheese

★ Slice Fritos bag in middle from top to bottom.

★ Pour warm chili inside bag over Fritos and top with shredded cheese. Get a spoon and you're set!

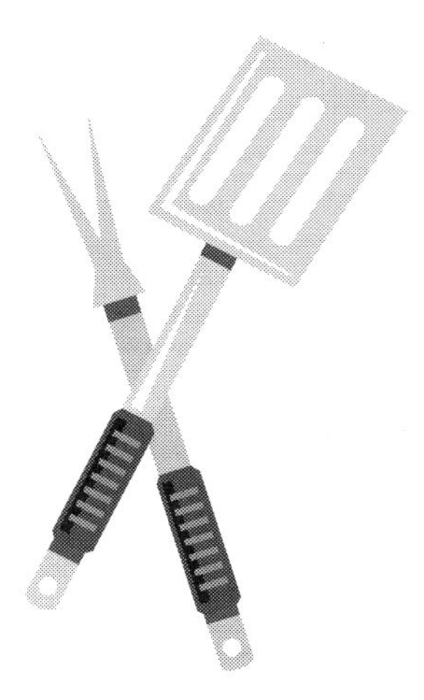

Mini-Pizza Faces

4 English muffins
1 (25 ounce) jar spaghetti sauce
1 cup shredded mozzarella cheese
$^1/_2$ cup shredded cheddar cheese
4 pepperoni slices, halved
8 black or green olives, halved

★ Cut English muffins and toast until well browned.

★ Spread each half with layer spaghetti sauce. Sprinkle with mozzarella cheese.

★ Make faces by sprinkling cheddar cheese at top of each muffin for hair. Arrange black olive slices for eyes and pepperoni slices for mouths.

★ Put muffins on a baking sheet and place under broiler for 1 to 2 minutes until cheese melts.

Neato Burritos

This is a great quick and tasty snack or lunch. Add seasoned taco meat with ingredients or go with it as is.

Flour tortillas
Refried beans
Shredded cheddar cheese
Picante sauce, optional
Sour cream, optional
Shredded lettuce, optional

★ Spread flour tortilla with refried beans.

★ Sprinkle cheese over beans.

★ Microwave for 30 to 45 seconds on HIGH power until cheese melts.

★ If desired, add picante sauce, sour cream and lettuce.

★ Roll burrito by folding one edge over filling, then folding one of the sides over and rolling up.

Part II:

Stuff You Want To Eat All The Time

Fruit Cookie Wedges

This is a great way to get kids to eat fruits. They can make their own designs and enjoy the fruits of their labor.

1 (18 ounce) package refrigerated sugar cookie dough
1 (3 ounce) package cream cheese, softened
1 (7 ounce) jar marshmallow cream
Assorted fresh fruit slices

- Preheat oven to 350°. Press sugar cookie dough into lightly greased pizza pan.
- Bake for 12 to 14 minutes or until golden brown. Remove from oven and cool.
- Mix cream cheese and marshmallow cream until blended. Spread evenly over cookie.
- Arrange fruit over cream cheese mixture in fun patterns like faces, spirals, circles or triangles.

Tip: To keep banana slices from turning brown, dip in pineapple juice before placing on cream cheese mixture.

Cookie Pizza

1 (18 ounce) package refrigerated sugar cookie dough
1 (16 ounce) carton white icing, tinted red
Candied cherries, halved
Green gumdrops
Circles cut from red fruit leather for pepperoni
Grated white chocolate for cheese

- Preheat oven to 350°.
- Spread cookie dough in ungreased pizza pan. Bake for 15 minutes or until lightly browned. Remove from oven and let cool.
- Spread red icing evenly over surface of cookie.
- Arrange candied cherry halves, gumdrop pieces and fruit roll-ups circles on top.
- Sprinkle grated white chocolate lightly over all and press down gently.
- Cut into slices and serve.

Cheesecake Grahams

1 (3 ounce) package cream cheese, softened
3 tablespoons strawberry preserves
4 whole graham crackers

- In small bowl combine cream cheese and strawberry preserves and blend well.
- Spread cream cheese mixture on graham crackers and cover each evenly.
- Make strawberry sandwich treats by putting fresh strawberry slices on cream cheese and cover with another graham cracker.

Church Window Cookies

1/4 cup (1/2 stick) butter or margarine
1 (12 ounce) package semi-sweet or milk chocolate chips
1 (10 ounce) package colored marshmallows
1 (14 ounce) package shredded coconut

- Put butter and chocolate chips in large microwave-safe bowl. Microwave on HALF power 1 minute at time, stirring after each minute, until chocolate and butter melts and mixture is smooth.
- Let mixture cool a little and stir in marshmallows.
- Put coconut in shallow plate or pan. Divide chocolate mixture in half and form 2 logs 2 1/2 -inches wide.
- Cover each roll with coconut and wrap in plastic.
- Refrigerate for 24 hours to chill thoroughly. Cut into 1/2-inch slices and serve.

Spider Cookies

1 (16 ounce) package chocolate chip cookies
1 (16 ounce) carton chocolate frosting
Black lace licorice, cut into 5-inch lengths
Chocolate coating

- ♥ Cover flat side of cookie with frosting.
- ♥ Place 3 licorice laces across cookie on top of frosting so they cross in middle and stick out of each side like legs.
- ♥ Frost flat side of another cookie with icing. Put frosting side down over "legs" of other cookies and gently press together. Repeat with remaining cookies.
- ♥ Melt chocolate coating as directed on the package.
- ♥ Place cookies on cooling rack with piece of waxed paper underneath to catch drips. Spoon chocolate coating over each cookie to coat it.
- ♥ Put 2 Red Hot candies or chocolate chips for eyes on wet chocolate coating.
- ♥ Let chocolate coating set before serving.

Hidden Caramel Cookies

These cookies look like ordinary sugar cookies from the outside, but.... surprise! The insides contain caramel and chocolate.

1 (18 ounce) package refrigerated sugar cookie dough
1 (14 ounce) package chocolate covered caramels

- Preheat oven to 350°.
- Slice dough about 1/4-inch thick. Take unwrapped caramel and put in center of each slice.
- Shape dough around caramel candy to completely enclose it. Place cookie on ungreased baking sheet.
- Bake for 10 to 12 minutes or until cookie is lightly browned.
- Remove cookies from oven and cool for 1 minute on baking sheet. Transfer to cooling rack to cool completely.

Chocolate Boulders

2 cups sugar
1/2 cup cocoa powder
1/2 cup milk
1/2 cup (1 stick) butter or margarine
1 teaspoon vanilla
3 cups quick-cooking oats

- Combine sugar, cocoa powder, milk, butter and vanilla in large, heavy saucepan. Turn heat to medium and let mixture come to a boil.
- Cook for 5 minutes, stirring mixture often.
- Remove saucepan from heat and stir in oats. Mix well.
- Drop heaping tablespoons of chocolate mixture onto wax paper to cool.

Bird's Nest Cookies

2 cups chow mein noodles
1 cup corn flakes, crushed
1 (12 ounce) package
white chocolate chips, melted
Small jelly beans

- Put the chow mein noodles and crushed corn flakes in large bowl.
- Melt white chocolate in heavy saucepan over very low heat. Stir as chips melt and mixture becomes smooth.
- Pour melted white chocolate over cereal and noodles. Mix thoroughly.
- Spread some butter or margarine on tablespoon, scoop out spoonfuls of mixture and drop on wax paper.
- Press back of spoon in middle to create "well" in center of each mound.
- Put 2 or 3 jelly beans in middle of hole for "eggs".

Orange Snowballs

$^1/_2$ cup (1 stick) butter or margarine, softened
1 (16 ounce) box powdered sugar
1 (12 ounce) package vanilla wafers, finely crushed
1 (6 ounce) can frozen orange juice concentrate, thawed
$1^1/_2$ cups shredded coconut

♥ Put softened butter, powdered sugar, crushed cookies and orange juice concentrate in large bowl and mix until thoroughly blended.

♥ Using a teaspoon, scoop mixture and roll into small balls. Roll balls in coconut.

♥ Place in covered container and refrigerate until ready to serve.

Makes 5 dozen.

Dirty Snowballs

This version of Orange Snowballs cookies has chocolate in it.

1 (9 ounce) package vanilla wafer cookies, crushed
2 1/4 cups powdered sugar, divided
1/4 cup unsweetened cocoa powder
1/3 cup frozen orange juice concentrate, thawed
1/4 cup light corn syrup

- Put wafers in sealed plastic bag and use rolling pin to crush them. Put crushed vanilla wafers, 2 cups powdered sugar, cocoa powder, orange juice concentrate and corn syrup in large bowl.

- Mix everything together until moistened. Scoop out some of mixture and roll into balls about 1-inch wide.

- Roll balls in remaining 1/4 cup powdered sugar. Store cookies in refrigerator in covered container.

Lip Lickin' Lemon Bites

This is an easy no-bake recipe.

3 cups (one 13.5 ounce) box graham cracker crumbs
1 cup powdered sugar, divided
1/4 cup frozen lemonade concentrate, thawed
3 tablespoons light corn syrup
3 tablespoons butter or margarine, melted

- ♥ Put graham cracker crumbs, 3/4 cup powdered sugar, orange juice concentrate, corn syrup and melted margarine in large bowl.
- ♥ Stir until mixture is completely blended. Take spoonfuls of mixture and shape into balls about 1-inch wide.
- ♥ Roll balls in remaining powdered sugar. You may also put cookies and remaining powdered sugar in sealed plastic bag and gently shake it.
- ♥ Store at room temperature.

Makes 3 dozen.

You may crush your own graham crackers by sealing them in plastic bag and crumbling them with rolling pin. You may buy graham cracker crumbs in box for the easiest and quickest way.

Chocolate-Covered Sandwich Cookies

These versatile cookies can be made to complement any holiday. For Christmas cookies, use white chocolate and colored sprinkles or crushed peppermint. For a "minty" middle, add 1/8 teaspoon peppermint extract and a few drops of green food coloring. For a Halloween look, add a few drops of red and yellow food coloring and flavor with 1/8 teaspoon orange extract. Need a sweet treat for Valentine's Day? Use white chocolate, sprinkles and red food coloring.

1 (16 ounce) carton chocolate frosting
72 butter-flavored crackers
1 (16 ounce) package chocolate candy coating
Candy sprinkles, optional

- Spread frosting on one cracker and put another cracker on top of frosting to make a sandwich cookie.
- Melt candy coating according to package directions. Place some large pieces of wax paper or aluminum foil on counter and dip or spoon cookies in chocolate.
- Place it on wax paper until the chocolate coating is dry.
- Sprinkle candy decorations over cookies before they dry.

Caramel Drop Cookies

This is an easy no-bake recipe.

2 cups packed brown sugar
$^1/_2$ cup (1 stick) butter or margarine
$^1/_2$ cup milk
3 cups quick-cooking oats
1 teaspoon vanilla

- Stir brown sugar, butter and milk in saucepan over medium heat until it comes to a boil.
- Continue to stir and boil mixture for 1 minute. Remove saucepan from heat and stir in oats and vanilla.
- Immediately, use tablespoon to scoop out spoonfuls of cookie mixture and drop onto wax paper. Cool.

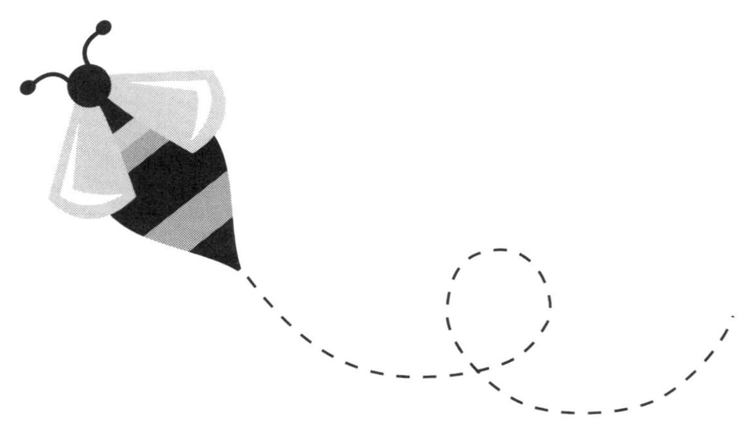

Cherry Surprise Cookies

Kids will love these chocolate-covered cookies with a surprise in the middle!

1 (18 ounce) package refrigerated sugar cookie dough
1 (10 ounce) jar maraschino cherries, drained, juice reserved
1 (6 ounce) package semi-sweet chocolate chips
½ cup sweetened condensed milk

- Preheat oven to 350°.
- Shape pieces of dough into 1-inch balls and place on ungreased baking sheet.
- Press center of dough with thumb to make an indentation. Place a cherry in the indentation.
- Combine chocolate and sweetened condensed milk in small, heavy saucepan over low heat. Cook and stir until chocolate melts.
- Add 4 teaspoons of reserved cherry juice to saucepan and stir until smooth.
- Spoon about 1 teaspoon chocolate mixture over each cherry and spread to cover completely. Place chocolate-covered cherry in cookie indentation
- Bake for 10 minutes. Remove from oven and let cookies cool on baking sheet for 1 minute. Transfer to cooling rack.

Candy Cane Cookies

$^{1}/_{2}$ cup (1 stick) butter or margarine, softened
1 cup sugar
1 egg
$^{1}/_{2}$ teaspoon vanilla
1 teaspoon peppermint extract
$^{1}/_{2}$ teaspoon salt
1 teaspoon baking powder
2 cups flour
Red food coloring

- ♥ In large bowl, cream butter and sugar. Add egg, vanilla and peppermint extract. Beat until light and fluffy.
- ♥ In medium bowl, sift salt, baking powder and flour together. Gradually add to butter mixture and beat well after each addition.
- ♥ Divide dough in half. Color half with several drops of red food coloring. Cover and refrigerate dough until ready to use.
- ♥ Preheat oven to 375°.
- ♥ Take teaspoonful of red dough and roll into a rope about 6-inches long. Take teaspoonful of uncolored dough and roll into log the same length.

(continued on next page)

(continued)

- Put two pieces next to each other and gently twist. (I generally lift one end and twist toward the middle as I lift the dough pieces. I then lift and twist the other end as I place it on the baking sheet.)
- Lift dough and place on baking sheet, shaping top half into crook shape for candy cane.
- Bake for 10 minutes and remove from oven.
- Let cookies cool on baking sheet for 1 minute. Transfer to cooling rack.

Snowman Cookies

Use gumdrops for hats, silver dragees or miniature chocolate-covered candies for buttons and miniature chocolate chips for eyes.

1 (8 ounce) package cream cheese, softened
1 cup powdered sugar
3/4 cup (1 1/2 sticks) butter or margarine
1/2 teaspoon vanilla
2 1/4 cups flour
1/2 teaspoon baking soda
3 tablespoons granulated sugar
Candies for decoration

- ♥ Preheat oven to 325°.
- ♥ Combine cream cheese, sugar, butter and vanilla in medium bowl. Beat with mixer on medium speed until well blended.
- ♥ Sift flour and baking soda together. Add to cream cheese mixture in several additions and beat well after each addition.
- ♥ Shape dough into balls 1/2-inch, 1-inch and 1 1/2-inches in diameter. Arrange balls with sides touching from smallest to largest (like a snowman) on ungreased baking sheet.

(continued on next page)

(continued)

- Flatten to 1/4-inch thickness with bottom of glass dipped in sugar. Repeat with remaining dough.
- Decorate cookies with colored candies to make buttons and eyes.
- Bake for 19 to 21 minutes or until light golden brown.
- Remove cookies from oven and let cool on baking sheet for 1 minute. Transfer to cooling rack.
- Sprinkle each snowman with sifted powdered sugar.
- Cut gumdrops in half and place cut side down on top of head for hat.

Gingerbread Cookie Bowls

Make fun and festive little gingerbread cookie bowls with cut- out edges using your favorite cookie dough. Kids will love eating out of these cookie bowls.

Favorite homemade or refrigerated cookie dough

- Preheat oven to 325°.
- Roll out dough to 1/4-inch thickness. Cut circles size of small oven-proof bowls.
- Turn bowls upside down on a baking sheet and shape dough circles over them.
- Leave dough over bowls and cut out shapes around rim and sides of dough with small cookie cutters.
- Place bowls with dough and cookie cut-outs on baking sheet. Bake for 20 to 25 minutes. (Check cookie cut-outs after about 10 to 15 minutes.)
- Remove from oven and let cool completely. Gently and carefully remove cookie bowls from their "molds."
- Fill with vanilla pudding topped with baked cookie cut-outs.

Cookie Pops

You may decorate these cookie lollipops in many ways. Before baking, sprinkle colored candy or colored sugar over them. After baking, dip them in melted chocolate or white candy coating tinted in favorite colors. To use as a take-to-school treat, cover each cookie with sandwich bag and close with piece of ribbon or colored pipe cleaner.

1 (18 ounce) package refrigerated cookie dough
Lollipop sticks or wooden craft sticks

♥ Preheat oven to 350°.

♥ Slice cookie dough into pieces about 1/4-inch thick and place 3 inches apart on ungreased baking sheet.

♥ Insert lollipop stick or wooden craft stick into each piece, pressing down gently.

♥ Bake for 10 to 12 minutes or until golden brown.

♥ Cool on baking sheets for 1 minute. Transfer cookies to wire racks to cool completely.

Watermelon Slices

Red food coloring
1 egg yolk
1/4 teaspoon water
1 (18 ounce) package refrigerated sugar cookie dough
1/4 cup green decorator sugar
1/2 cup mini-chocolate chips

- Preheat oven to 350°.
- Combine food coloring with egg yolk and water and mix well. Set aside.
- Cut sugar cookie dough into slices about 1/4-inch thick. Cut rounds in half to make two wedges and dip edge of round side of each wedge in green sugar to make "rind".
- Using soft pastry brush, dip brush into egg yolk mixture and brush unsugared cookie surface lightly to make it pink.
- Place cookie wedges 3 inches apart on ungreased baking sheet. Gently press 4 or 5 chocolate chips into pink part of cookie to make "seeds". Bake for 8 to 10 minutes.
- Remove from oven and let cookies cool on baking sheet for 1 minute. Transfer to cooling rack.

To color your own sugar, mix 2 to 3 drops green food coloring into 1/4 cup sugar. Stir until all sugar is evenly colored.

Cookie Rainbows

1 (8 ounce) package refrigerated sugar cookie dough
4 assorted food colorings

- Preheat oven to 375°.
- Divide dough into 4 sections and add a few drops food coloring to each section. Blend well.
- On wax paper, form each dough section into an 8 x 4-inch rectangle about 1/4-inch thick.
- Stack rectangles on top of each other, cover and refrigerate for a few hours to chill.
- Cut rectangle on the short end into 1/4-inch slices and gently shape into arches. Place 2 inches apart on an ungreased baking sheet and bake for 7 minutes or until very lightly browned.

Painted Butterfly Cookies

1 (18 ounce) package refrigerated sugar cookie dough
1 egg yolk
$^1/_4$ teaspoon water
Assorted food colors

- Preheat oven at 350°.
- Slice cookie dough into pieces about $^1/_2$-inch thick.
- Cut 1 slice in half and arrange two halves with their rounded sides next to each other spaced about $^1/_2$ inch apart on ungreased baking sheet to make "wings".
- Take half another slice of dough and shape into rope about 2 inches long for body. Place between wings.
- Use knife to make small cut in straight side of each "wing" to separate slightly.
- Mix egg yolk with water in small bowl. Divide egg yolk mixture between several small containers, one for each color. Add several drops of one food coloring to each and mix well.
- Use small craft paint brush to paint cookies with egg yolk mixture. (Use one for each color or be sure to wash the brush well before using another color.)
- Bake for 12 to 14 minutes or until light golden brown. Remove from oven and let cookies cool on baking sheet for 1 minute. Transfer to cooling rack.

Fast Chocolate Haystacks

4 (1 ounce) squares unsweetened chocolate, melted
1 (14 ounce) can sweetened condensed milk
2 teaspoons vanilla
1 (14 ounce) package shredded coconut

- Preheat oven at 350°.
- In large bowl, combine chocolate, sweetened condensed milk and vanilla. Stir until well blended and evenly colored. Stir in coconut.
- Drop by heaping teaspoonfuls about 2 inches apart onto greased baking sheet. Bake for 10 minutes.
- Remove from oven and immediately transfer to cooling rack.

Makes 3 1/2 dozen.

Snickerdoodle Bears

1 (18 ounce) package refrigerated sugar cookie dough
4 tablespoons sugar
4 tablespoons cinnamon
Raisins

- Preheat oven to 375°.
- For each bear, shape sugar cookie dough into 1 large ball for body, 1 medium ball for head and 6 small ones for arms, legs and ears.
- Combine sugar and cinnamon in shallow dish and mix well. Roll each ball in the cinnamon-sugar mixture.
- Place 1 large ball for the body on lightly greased baking sheet. Put 1 medium ball just above it with sides touching for the head.
- Place 2 small balls on top of head for ears and place 4 small balls around body for arms and legs.
- Put two raisins on head for eyes and one in middle of the body for the button.
- Bake for 15 minutes. Remove from oven and let cookies cool for 1 minute. Transfer to cooling rack.

Almost Instant Chocolate Cookies

I believe that "no-bake cookies" were one of the first recipes I ever made. I remember getting the recipe at school and I couldn't wait to get home to try it. They were a big hit at our house and after that all the kids were making them. They are fast, easy and use ingredients that are usually in the pantry.

1½ cups sugar
½ cup (1 stick) butter or margarine
½ cup milk
½ cup cocoa powder
1 teaspoon vanilla
3½ cups quick-cooking oats
1 cup shredded coconut

- ♥ Line several baking sheets with wax paper or just place several long sheets on countertop.
- ♥ Combine sugar, butter, milk and cocoa in saucepan over medium heat.
- ♥ Cook, stirring constantly, until mixture begins to boil.
- ♥ Remove from heat and stir in vanilla, oats and coconut.
- ♥ Working quickly, drop rounded teaspoonfuls of mixture onto wax paper. Let cool and enjoy.

Kat-Face Kookies

Kids love making faces on these cookies before they are baked.

1 (18 ounce) package refrigerated chocolate chip cookie dough
1/3 cup (72) small round M & M candies
48 (2 1/2-inch) thin pretzel sticks, halved

- Freeze cookie dough for 1 hour.
- Preheat oven at 350°.
- Slice cookie dough into 24 pieces. Place each slice 3 inches apart on ungreased baking sheet.
- Place 3 candy pieces on each cookie for eyes and nose. (Use the same color for the eyes and a different color for the nose.)
- Arrange several pretzel pieces on each side of nose to make whiskers and press down lightly.
- Bake for 11 to 13 minutes or until golden brown. Cool for 1 minute and transfer to cooling rack.

No-Bake Bars

2 eggs, beaten
1 cup sugar
3/4 cup (1 1/2 sticks) butter or margarine
1 teaspoon vanilla
2 1/2 cups miniature marshmallows
30 graham crackers, crushed
1 cup shredded coconut

- ♥ Combine eggs, sugar and butter in heavy saucepan over medium heat. Cook, stirring constantly, until thickened. Remove from heat and cool.
- ♥ Stir in vanilla, marshmallows, graham crackers and coconut.
- ♥ Press into buttered 9 x 13-inch baking pan and refrigerate to chill.
- ♥ Cut into bars and serve.

Banana Cookie Bars

Here's an easy microwave recipe for delicious bars.

16 (1 1/2-inch) square shortbread cookies
1 (16 ounce) carton vanilla frosting, divided
1 banana, mashed
3/4 cup biscuit baking mix
1 egg

- Arrange shortbread cookies in single layer in bottom of glass baking dish.
- Measure 1 cup frosting from carton and set aside.
- Measure 1/2 cup frosting and put in bowl. Add mashed banana to frosting in bowl and mix with fork until smooth.
- Beat biscuit baking mix and egg until batter is blended.
- Spread batter evenly over cookies in baking dish. Cover dish with wax paper and microwave on HIGH for 2 minutes.

(continued on next page)

(continued)

- Turn dish 1/2 turn and microwave another 3 minutes or until a toothpick inserted in center comes out clean.
- Carefully lift edge of wax paper farthest away from you to let steam out and remove wax paper.
- Remove dish from microwave and place on cooling rack. Let bars cool completely and frost with remaining frosting. Cut into squares.

Cherry Crumb Bars

1 (18.25 ounce) box white cake mix
$^1/_2$ cup (1 stick) butter or margarine, softened, divided
1$^1/_4$ cups rolled quick-cooking oats, divided
1 egg
1 (21 ounce) can cherry pie filling
$^1/_4$ cup packed brown sugar

- Preheat oven to 350°.
- Combine cake mix, 6 tablespoons butter and 1 cup rolled oats. Mix until crumbly. Reserve 1 cup for topping.
- Add egg to remaining mixture and blend well. Press into greased, floured, 9 x 13-inch baking pan.
- Spread cherry filling evenly over mixture in pan.
- In large bowl, combine remaining 1 cup crumb mixture with remaining $^1/_4$ cup oats, 2 tablespoons butter and brown sugar. Mix well. Sprinkle over cherries.
- Bake for 30 to 40 minutes or until top is browned.

Strawberry Jam Bars

1 cup flour
1 cup rolled or quick-cooking oats
1/3 cup packed brown sugar
1/4 teaspoon baking powder
1/8 teaspoon salt
1/2 cup (1 stick) butter or margarine, softened
3/4 cup strawberry jam

- ♥ Preheat oven at 350°.
- ♥ In large bowl, combine flour, oats, brown sugar, baking powder and salt. Stir to mix.
- ♥ Cut butter into dry mixture until it is moist and crumbly.
- ♥ Remove 2 cups oat mixture and press evenly into bottom of ungreased 9 x 13-inch baking pan.
- ♥ Using spatula or back of large spoon, carefully spread strawberry jam evenly over mixture in pan to within 1/4-inch of pan's edge.
- ♥ Sprinkle remaining oat mixture lightly over strawberry jam and gently press down.
- ♥ Bake for 25 minutes or until top is lightly browned. Remove from oven and let cool. Cut into squares.

White Chocolate Bars

1 (18.25 ounce) box French vanilla or white cake mix
$^{1}/_{3}$ cup butter or margarine
2 tablespoons water
1 teaspoon vanilla
1 egg
$1^{1}/_{2}$ cups shredded coconut
$^{1}/_{2}$ cup white chocolate chips

♥ Preheat oven to 350°.

♥ Combine cake mix and butter in large mixing bowl. Cut in butter using fork or pastry cutter until mixture is crumbly.

♥ Add water, vanilla and egg and mix well. Stir in coconut.

♥ Press dough into greased 9 x 13-inch baking pan.

♥ Bake for 15 to 20 minutes or until golden brown. Remove from oven and let cool for 15 minutes.

♥ Melt chocolate in saucepan and drizzle over cake. Cool and cut into bars.

Easy Raisin Bars

3 eggs
1 cup sugar
1 teaspoon vanilla
1 teaspoon baking powder
1 cup flour
1 cup raisins
1/4 cup powdered sugar

- Preheat oven to 350°.
- In medium bowl, beat eggs, sugar and vanilla.
- Mix in baking powder and flour.
- Stir in raisins. (Batter will be thick.)
- Pour into greased 8 x 8-inch baking dish and bake for 25 to 30 minutes.
- Remove from oven and cool. Sprinkle powdered sugar over top.

Cheddar-Apple Granola Bars

These are healthy and great snacks.

2 cups flour
1 teaspoon baking powder
$^{1}/_{2}$ teaspoon salt
$2^{1}/_{2}$ cups granola, divided
2 cups shredded cheddar cheese, divided
$^{3}/_{4}$ cup applesauce
$^{1}/_{4}$ cup apple juice concentrate
$^{1}/_{4}$ cup cooking oil
2 eggs

- Preheat oven to 375°
- Combine flour, baking powder and salt in large bowl. Stir in 2 cups granola and $1^{1}/_{2}$ cups cheese.
- In another bowl, whisk together applesauce, apple juice concentrate, oil and eggs.
- Stir mixture into dry ingredients until well blended.
- Spread batter in lightly-greased 9 x 13-inch baking pan.
- Preheat oven to 375°.
- Sprinkle top with remaining $^{1}/_{2}$ cup shredded cheese and $^{1}/_{2}$ cup granola.
- Bake 20 to 30 minutes or until edges are lightly browned. Cool and cut into bars.

Sunshine Bars

1 (18 ounce) package refrigerated sugar cookie dough
3 eggs
1½ cups sugar
3 tablespoons flour
¼ cup fresh lemon juice
⅓ cup powdered sugar

- Preheat oven to 375°. Press cookie dough into bottom of ungreased 9 x 13-inch baking pan.
- Bake for 20 minutes or until slightly golden. While crust is baking, whisk together eggs, sugar, flour and lemon juice until frothy.
- Pour lemon mixture over hot crust.
- Return to oven for additional 20 to 25 minutes or until light golden brown.
- Cool on a wire rack.
- Dust top with powdered sugar. Cut into squares.

Caramel-Cereal Crisps

1/4 cup (1/2 stick) butter or margarine
1 tablespoon light corn syrup
1 cup packed dark brown sugar
1 tablespoon water
1/4 teaspoon salt
3 1/2 cups crisp rice cereal

- Combine butter and corn syrup in heavy saucepan over low heat. Cook until butter melts.
- Stir in sugar, water and salt. Cook, stirring constantly, until mixture begins to boil.
- Boil for 3 minutes.
- Without removing from heat, add cereal and stir until evenly coated.
- Quickly spread mixture into buttered 13 x 9-inch pan.
- Score into bars while still soft. When cool, turn candy from pan and break into pieces along score lines.

Brownie Christmas Trees

1 (8 x 8-inch) or (9 x 9-inch) pan brownies, baked, uncut
Small peppermint sticks for each brownie "tree"
1 (16 ounce) carton vanilla icing
Green food coloring
Red Hot candies
Red gel icing

- Cut brownies into 4 equal squares, cut each square diagonally to form 2 triangles, making 8 triangles.
- Insert peppermint stick into widest part of triangle tree for "trunk."
- Tint vanilla icing with green food coloring.
- Ice each brownie with green icing and decorate with Red Hots or small candies for ornaments.
- Use red gel icing in a zig-zag pattern to make garlands on each tree.
- Other colorful candy-coated chocolate candies, such as M & M's and skittles, or colorful gumdrops work well also. Us your imagination to make beautiful Christmas trees.

Colored Sugar & Coconut for Decorating Cookies and Cakes

Make your own colored sugar or coconut to sprinkle.

Sugar
Food coloring

- Take about 1/4 cup sugar for each color and add 2 to 3 drops of food coloring. Stir until sugar is evenly colored.
- Repeat with as many colors as you want.
- Store in airtight container.

Coconut
Food coloring

- For 1/2 cup shredded coconut, sprinkle about 2 to 3 drops of desired food coloring.
- Stir until well blended.
- Store in airtight container.

Spider Cupcakes

Prepared cupcakes
Chocolate frosting
Red Hot candies for eyes
Black licorice lace for legs
Red licorice lace for mouths

Frost cupcakes and put 2 Red Hot candies on top for eyes.

Use small piece of red licorice lace for mouth and place under eyes.

For legs, cut pieces of black licorice lace into $2^1/_2$-inch sections. Insert about $^1/_2$-inch laces into edge of cupcake and put about 3 or 4 on each side.

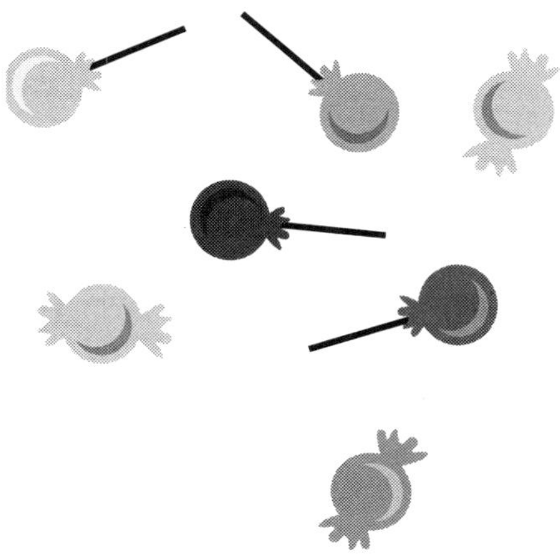

Chocolate Surprise Cupcakes

These are great for school parties because you don't have icing to worry about. For a decorative touch, create designs on top in powdered sugar by using small stencils. You can find stencils in craft stores with the baking supplies.

1 (8 ounce) package cream cheese, softened
1/3 cup sugar
1 egg
1/2 cup semi-sweet chocolate chips, melted
1 (18.25 ounce) chocolate cake mix
1/4 cup sifted powdered sugar

Preheat oven to 350°.

Prepare cake mix according to package directions, but do not bake.

In medium bowl, beat cream cheese, sugar and egg until smooth. Stir in chocolate and set aside.

Spoon half the cake batter evenly into 18 partially filled, greased or paper-lined muffin cups. Top each with 1 tablespoon cream cheese mixture.

Spoon remaining batter evenly over cream cheese mixture.

Bake for 30 to 35 minutes or until toothpick inserted into center comes out clean.

Remove cupcakes from pans to cool on wire racks. Sprinkle with powdered sugar.

Easter Basket Cupcakes

1-1 1/2 dozen baked, unfrosted cupcakes
1 (16 ounce) carton white frosting
1-2 drops green food coloring
1 cup shredded coconut
36-50 "Robin's eggs" or jelly bean eggs
12-18 strawberry licorice sticks

♥ Generously frost cupcakes with white frosting, but reserve a few tablespoonfuls of icing to attach eggs to cupcake tops.

♥ Color coconut green by stirring in food coloring until it is completely colored.

♥ Sprinkle green coconut on cupcakes and gently press into frosting to make it stick.

♥ Place small dab of icing in center of each cupcake and put several eggs on top. Press down gently but firmly into icing.

♥ Insert ends of licorice into each side of cupcake, one directly across from other, to form handles. (You may need to cut sticks into short pieces to make handles right size.)

Christmas "Ice Cream Cones"

1 (18.25 ounce) box white cake mix
10 drops red food coloring
30 flat bottom ice cream cones
1 (16 ounce) tub vanilla frosting
1 cup crushed peppermint candy canes

- Preheat oven to 350°.
- Prepare cake mix as directed on box, but add red food coloring to batter before beating.
- Place cones about 3 inches apart on ungreased baking sheet and fill each ice cream cone with about $2\frac{1}{2}$ tablespoons of batter. Bake for 25 to 30 minutes.
- Cool completely. Ice each cupcake with vanilla frosting and immediately decorate with crushed candy.

Apple-Cinnamon Muffins

1 egg
2 cups biscuit and baking mix
3/4 cup applesauce
1/3 cup sugar
2/3 cup milk
2 tablespoons cooking oil
2 teaspoons cinnamon

- Preheat oven to 400°.
- Grease bottom only of 12 muffin cups or line them with paper liners.
- Beat egg slightly and add biscuit mix, applesauce, sugar, milk, oil and cinnamon. Stir just until moistened.
- Divide batter evenly between muffin cups.
- Bake for 15 to 17 minutes until muffins are golden brown.

Makes 12 muffins.

Banana Muffins

This is a healthy, tasty treat.

½ cup (1 stick) butter or margarine, softened
½ cup sugar
2 eggs
1 cup ripe mashed bananas
¾ cup honey
1½ cups flour
1 cup quick-cooking oats
1 teaspoon baking powder
1 teaspoon baking soda
¾ teaspoon salt

- Preheat oven at 350°.
- Cream butter and sugar together in large bowl.
- Stir in eggs, bananas and honey and blend well.
- Sift together flour, oats, baking powder, baking soda and salt. Stir into banana mixture until moistened.
- Fill greased or paper-lined muffin cups two-thirds full.
- Bake for 18 to 20 minutes or until knife inserted in center comes out clean.
- Remove from oven and cool.

Makes 18 muffins.

Erupting Volcano Cake

1 unfrosted Bundt cake
Several drops red food coloring
2 ounces frozen whipped topping, thawed
1 (20 ounce) can cherry pie filling
3-4 chocolate sandwich cookies, crushed

- Put cake onto serving platter.
- Add food coloring to whipped topping and blend well. Fill hole in center of cake with colored topping.
- Put cherry pie filling for lava on top of whipped topping and drizzle some of it down the cake's sides.
- Sprinkle top and sides of volcano with crushed cookie crumbs.

Homemade Ice Cream Sandwiches

16 large chocolate chip cookies
1 quart ice cream, softened slightly

- Soften ice cream. Spread about 1/2 cup ice cream on flat side of 8 cookies.
- Place another cookie, flat side down, over ice cream and gently press together. Repeat with remaining 8 cookies.
- Take tip of butter knife and run it around sides of the sandwich to smooth out ice cream. Wrap sandwiches individually in plastic wrap or foil and freeze until ice cream is firm.

Makes 8 sandwiches.

Cannoli Cones

Here is a great quick and easy way to have cannoli. For a really nice presentation, melt a cup of chocolate chips and stir until smooth. Dip the mouth of the ice cream cone in it so it covers about 1 or 2 inches. Refrigerate to set the chocolate.

½ teaspoon grated orange peel
1 (15 ounce) container ricotta cheese
⅔ cup powdered sugar
½ teaspoon vanilla
2 tablespoons miniature chocolate chips
10 sugar ice cream cones

- Put orange peel, ricotta cheese, sugar and vanilla in large bowl. Beat with hand mixer on low speed until mixture is smooth.
- Stir in chocolate chips. Cover mixture and refrigerate for 30 minutes.
- When ready to serve cones, spoon some cheese mixture into each cone.

Apple Crisp

2 apples, peeled, cored, sliced into 1/4-inch pieces
1/4 cup quick-cooking oats
1/4 cup flour
1/4 cup packed brown sugar
4 tablespoons (1/2 stick) butter or margarine, softened
1/4 teaspoon ground cinnamon

- ♥ Put apple slices in glass 8 x 8-inch baking dish or 8-inch round cake pan.
- ♥ Place oats, flour, brown sugar and butter in bowl and mix well.
- ♥ Sprinkle mixture evenly over apples.
- ♥ Microwave uncovered on HIGH for 6 minutes or until apples are tender when pierced with fork.
- ♥ Remove baking dish from microwave and cool uncovered for 10 minutes.

Peppermint Party Pie

This is a great way to use up leftover Christmas candy canes. To crush candy canes without making a big mess, seal them in a plastic bag and gently pound candy with rolling pin or hammer.

1 cup whipping cream
1 cup crushed peppermint candy, divided
1 cup miniature marshmallows
1 (6 ounce) chocolate pie crust

- ♥ Whip cream in medium bowl by beating on high speed until peaks form.
- ♥ Add ³/₄ cup crushed candy to whipped cream and mix well. Stir in marshmallows.
- ♥ Spread mixture in pie crust. Sprinkle remaining ¹/₄ cup peppermint candy over top for decoration. Chill until ready to serve.

Gold Mine Pie

Dig into this lemony pie and you'll be surprised to find little nuggets of lemon candy.

1 (12 ounce) carton frozen whipped topping, thawed
1 (6 ounce) package lemon-flavored gelatin
2 (8 ounce) cartons lemon yogurt
½ cup coarsely crushed lemon drops
2 (6 ounce) prepared graham cracker crusts

♥ Put whipped topping in large bowl and sprinkle lemon gelatin over it. Beat on low speed with hand mixer until well blended.

♥ Stir in yogurt and lemon candy and mix well.

♥ Spoon half of mixture into one crust and half the mixture into the other crust. Cover and refrigerate for several hours before serving.

To crush candy without making a big mess, seal it in a plastic bag and gently pound candy with rolling pin or hammer.

Black and White Pie

2 cups crushed chocolate sandwich cookies, divided
1 (6 ounce) prepared chocolate pie crust
2 large bananas, divided
1 cup whipping cream or whipped topping
2 tablespoons sugar

- Sprinkle 1 cup crushed cookies into pie crust and smooth out.

- Slice 1 banana and place slices on top of cookies. Beat whipping cream with sugar and spread half of it or half whipped topping over bananas.

- Sprinkle remaining cookies over whipped cream. Slice remaining banana, put slices on cookies and cover with remaining whipped cream.

Autumn Harvest Pie

Here is a great no-bake Thanksgiving pie.

1 (3.4 ounce) package instant vanilla pudding mix
1 (16 ounce) can pumpkin
1 cup milk
1 teaspoon pumpkin pie spice
1 (4 ounce) carton frozen whipped topping, thawed, divided
1 (9 inch) graham cracker crumb crust

- ♥ Put pudding mix, pumpkin, milk and pie spice in large bowl. Beat until mixture is blended.
- ♥ Stir in 1 cup whipped topping. Spoon mixture into pie crust.
- ♥ Chill for about 2 hours. Before serving, top each slice with remaining whipped topping.

Easy Mints

You can color coordinate these easy mints to match whatever holiday you are celebrating. You can divide the mint mixture in half and color one half green and the other red for Christmas. Color one half pink and the other red for Valentine's day or make pretty pastel colors for Easter.

1/3 cup butter, softened
1/3 cup light corn syrup
1/2 teaspoon salt
1 teaspoon peppermint extract
3 1/2 cups (16 ounces) powdered sugar
Food coloring

- ♥ Combine butter, corn syrup, salt and peppermint extract in large bowl. Cream together until smooth.
- ♥ Add powdered sugar a little at a time until mixture is stiff. Knead with your hands until well blended.
- ♥ Divide mixture evenly into sections. Add a few drops of food coloring to each section to color it. Mix well.
- ♥ Take small pieces of mint mixture and roll into balls, press ball lightly with fork to make a design. To make cute Easter "eggs", roll 1 side of ball gently with fingers to elongate it and make an egg shape.
- ♥ Cover and refrigerate mints for 30 minutes or until firm. Keep refrigerated until serving time.

Fudge In A Flash

1 (12 ounce) package semi-sweet chocolate chips
1 (14 ounce) can sweetened condensed milk

- ♥ Grease 8-inch square pan and set aside.
- ♥ Place chocolate chips and sweetened condensed milk in medium saucepan over medium-low heat. Cook and stir constantly until chocolate melts and mixture is smooth and thick.
- ♥ Pour into pan and cool.
- ♥ To microwave put chocolate chips and sweetened condensed milk in large microwave-safe, 2-quart baking dish.
- ♥ Microwave on MEDIUM power for 3 minutes, stirring after 2 minutes.
- ♥ Microwave again on HALF power, stirring at 1 minute intervals, until chocolate melts and mixture is smooth and thick.

Variation: If you want cherry-flavored fudge, stir a 3-ounce package cherry gelatin into the sweetened condensed milk before adding chocolate.

Minute Mints

This is a really easy no-cook recipe.

1 (8 ounce) package cream cheese, softened
2 teaspoons peppermint extract
1 (2 pound) package powdered sugar
Food coloring

- Put cream cheese and peppermint flavoring in large bowl and mix well. Add powdered sugar a little at a time and mix well.
- To color mints, add a few drops of food coloring and mix. (If you want more than one color, divide mint mixture into batches and add a different color to each batch.)
- Take pieces of mixture and roll into little balls about the size of a dime. Flatten each with tip of fork and keep covered in refrigerator.

Index

D

E

F

Index

R

S

T

Pan Sizes

Pan Sizes	Approximate Volume
Muffin Pans	
1 ¾ x ¾ mini	⅛ cup (2 tablespoons)
2 ¾ x 1 ⅛	¼ cup
2 ¾ x 1 ⅜	Scant ½ cup
3 x 1 ¼ jumbo	⅝ cup
Loaf Pans	
5 ½ x 3 x 2 ½	2 cups
6 x 4 ½ x 3	3 cups
8 x 4 x 2 ½	4 cups
8 ½ x 4 ¼ x 3	5 cups
9 x 5 x 3	8 cups
Casseroles	
8 x 8 x 12 square	8 cups
11 x 7 x 2 rectangular	8 cups
9 x 9 x 2 square	10 cups
13 x 9 x 2 rectangular	15 cups
1-quart casserole	4 cups
2-quart casserole	8 cups
2 ½-quart casserole	10 cups
3-quart casserole	12 cups

Pan Sizes	Approximate Volume
Cake Pans	
5 x 2 round	2 ⅔ cups
6 x 2 round	3 ¾ cups
8 x 1 ½ round	4 cups
7 x 2 round	5 ¼ cups
8 x 2 round	6 cups
9 x 1 ½ round	6 cups
9 x 2 round	8 cups
9 x 3 bundt	9 cups
10 x 3 ½ bundt	12 cups
9 ½ x 2 ½ springform	10 cups
10 x 2 ½ springform	12 cups
8 x 3 tube	9 cups
9 x 4 tube	11 cups
10 x 4 tube	16 cups
Pie Pans	
7 x 1 ¼	2 cups
8 x 1 ¼	3 cups
8 x 1 ½	4 cups
9 x 1 ¼	4 cups
9 x 1 ½	5 cups
10 x 2	6 cups

U.S. Measurements

3 teaspoons	1 tablespoon	
4 tablespoons	¼ cup	2 fluid ounces
8 tablespoons	½ cup	4 fluid ounces
12 tablespoons	¾ cup	6 fluid ounces
16 tablespoons	1 cup	8 fluid ounces
¼ cup	4 tablespoons	2 fluid ounces
⅓ cup	5 tablespoons + 1 teaspoon	
½ cup	8 tablespoons	4 fluid ounces
⅔ cup	10 tablespoons + 2 teaspoons	
¾ cup	12 tablespoons	6 fluid ounces
1 cup	16 tablespoons	8 fluid ounces
1 cup	½ pint	
2 cups	1 pint	16 fluid ounces
3 cups	1 ½ pints	24 fluid ounces
4 cups	1 quart	32 fluid ounces
8 cups	2 quarts	64 fluid ounces
1 pint	2 cups	16 fluid ounces
2 pints	1 quart	
1 quart	2 pints; 4 cups	32 fluid ounces
4 quarts	1 gallon; 8 pints; 16 cups	
8 quarts	1 peck	
4 pecks	1 bushel	

Cookbooks Published By Cookbook Resources

Easy Cooking With 5 Ingredients
The Ultimate Cooking With 4 Ingredients
The Best of Cooking With 3 Ingredients
Easy Gourmet Cooking With 5 Ingredients
Healthy Cooking With 4 Ingredients
Easy Slow-Cooker Cooking With 4 Ingredients
Easy Dessert Cooking With 5 Ingredients
Quick Fixes With Mixes
Casseroles To The Rescue
Kitchen Keepsakes/More Kitchen Keepsakes
Mother's Recipes
Recipe Keepsakes
Cookie Dough Secrets
Gifts For The Cookie Jar
Cookbook 25 Years
Pass The Plate
Texas Longhorn Cookbook
Mealtimes and Memories
Holiday Treats
Homecoming
Cookin' With Will Rogers
Best of Lone Star Legacy Cookbook
Little Taste of Texas
Little Taste of Texas II
Southwest Sizzler
Southwest Ole
Classroom Treats
Leaving Home

www.cookbookresources.com

To Order **Class Treats**:

Please send______ copies @ $14.95 (U.S.) each $__________
Plus postage/handling @ $6.00 each $__________
Texas residents add sales tax @ $1.08 each $__________
Check or Credit Card (Canada-credit card only) **Total** $__________

Charge to my ❑ VISA or ❑ MasterCard

Account #______________________________
Expiration Date______________________________
Signature______________________________

Mail or Call:
Cookbook Resources
541 Doubletree Drive
Highland Village, TX 75077
Toll-free: 866/229-2665
972/317-0245
www.cookbookresources.com

Name____
Address____
City______________________________State__________Zip______________
Phone (day)______________________ (night)______________________

- -

To Order **Class Treats**:

Please send______ copies @ $14.95 (U.S.) each $__________
Plus postage/handling @ $6.00 each $__________
Texas residents add sales tax @ $1.08 each $__________
Check or Credit Card (Canada-credit card only) **Total** $__________

Charge to my ❑ VISA or ❑ MasterCard

Account #______________________________
Expiration Date______________________________
Signature______________________________

Mail or Call:
Cookbook Resources
541 Doubletree Drive
Highland Village, TX 75077
Toll-free: 866/229-2665
972/317-0245
www.cookbookresources.com

Name____
Address____
City______________________________State__________Zip______________
Phone (day)______________________ (night)______________________